Daniel Tiger's Day and Night

Adapted by Alexandra Cassel
Poses and layouts by Jason Fruchter

Simon Spotlight
New York   London   Toronto   Sydney   New Delhi

SIMON SPOTLIGHT
An imprint of Simon & Schuster Children's Publishing Division
1230 Avenue of the Americas, New York, New York 10020
This Simon Spotlight paperback edition December 2017
© 2017 The Fred Rogers Company
All rights reserved, including the right of reproduction in whole or in part in any form.
SIMON SPOTLIGHT and colophon are registered trademarks of Simon & Schuster, Inc.
For information about special discounts for bulk purchases, please contact Simon & Schuster
Special Sales at 1-866-506-1949 or business@simonandschuster.com.
Manufactured in the United States of America 1117 LAK
10 9 8 7 6 5 4 3 2 1
ISBN 978-1-5344-1176-0 (pbk)
ISBN 978-1-5344-1177-7 (eBook)

It's a beautiful day in the neighborhood, but Daniel is still in bed.

Dad Tiger says, "Wake up, Daniel Tiger. Wake up, sleepyhead!"

"Aaaaauh," Daniel yawns. "Good morning to YOU.

Will you help me get ready? I have so much to do!"

It's time to get ready for a grr-ific day!
What does Daniel need to do before it's time to play?

♪ *"Clothes on, eat breakfast, brush teeth,*
put on shoes, and off to school." ♪♪

First, he changes out of his pj's and into his clothes. The red sweater is his favorite, everyone knows.

Now that Daniel is dressed, what's next on the checklist? Let's go to the kitchen and see what's for breakfast.

Oatmeal with blueberries! Daniel's favorite treat. It smells delicious. What do YOU like to eat?

Next, he brushes his teeth until the timer dings.
"*Brusha, brusha, brush,*" Daniel Tiger sings.

DING!

Last, Daniel puts on his shoes before going outside. Trolley is here! Time to go for a ride.

Some days Daniel goes to the park for a picnic on the grass.

Some days he helps his dad at the store or goes to music class.

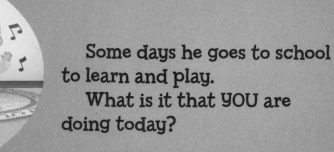

Some days he goes to school to learn and play.

What is it that YOU are doing today?

When the sun goes down and the moon shines bright, Daniel Tiger gets ready for night.

"That was a yummy dinner," Daniel said.

♪ "Now it's bathtime, pj's, brush teeth, story and song, and off to bed." ♪

Daniel loves bathtime. He gets into the tub.
He splashes in the bubbles. Scrub-a-dub-dub.

After the bath, what do we wear?
Pajamas, of course! Can you find his favorite pair?

To keep his teeth healthy and bright, Daniel brushes both day and night.

Daniel gets comfy and cozy in bed.
He reads a story, sings a song, and rests his tired head.

"It's time to sleep. The day is done.
Let's count down to calm down. 5, 4, 3, 2, 1."

Daniel holds Tigey and hugs him tight.
It is time to say goodnight.